A WORDFUL CHILD

by

George Ella Lyon

photographs by

Ann W. Olson

Richard C. Owen Publishers, Inc.
Katonah, New York

Meet the Author titles

Verna Aardema *A Bookworm Who Hatched*
Eve Bunting *Once Upon a Time*
Lois Ehlert *Under My Nose*
Jean Fritz *Surprising Myself*
Paul Goble *Hau Kola Hello Friend*
Ruth Heller *Fine Lines*
Lee Bennett Hopkins *The Writing Bug*
James Howe *Playing with Words*

Karla Kuskin *Thoughts, Pictures, and Words*
George Ella Lyon *A Wordful Child*
Margaret Mahy *My Mysterious World*
Rafe Martin *A Storyteller's Story*
Patricia Polacco *Firetalking*
Cynthia Rylant *Best Wishes*
Jane Yolen *A Letter from Phoenix Farm*

Text copyright © 1996 by George Ella Lyon
Photographs copyright © 1996 by Ann W. Olson

Richard C. Owen Publishers, Inc.
PO Box 585
Katonah, New York 10536

Library of Congress Cataloging-in-Publication Data

Lyon , George Ella .
     A wordful child / by George Ella Lyon : photographs by Ann W. Olson .
     p .   cm . — Meet the author (Katonah , N . Y .)
     Summary: The author describes how her love of words and her personal experiences evolved into a career as a writer.
     ISBN 1-57274-016-7 :
     1 . Lyon , George Ella , 1949- — Biography — Juvenile literature .
2 . Women authors , American — 20th century — Biography — Juvenile literature . 3 . Children's literature — Authorship — Juvenile literature . [1 . Lyon , George Ella , 1949- . 2 . Authors , American . 3 . Women — Biography .] I . Series : Meet the author
PS3562. Y4454Z469 1996
813' .54 — dc20
[B]

96-866
CIP
AC

Editorial, Art, and Production Director *Janice Boland*
Production Assistant *Matthew Vartabedian*
Color separations by Leo P. Callahan Inc., Binghamton, NY

Printed in the United States of America

9 8 7 6 5 4 3 2 1

To my readers,
for your words

I was a wordful child.
My family says I talked before I walked.

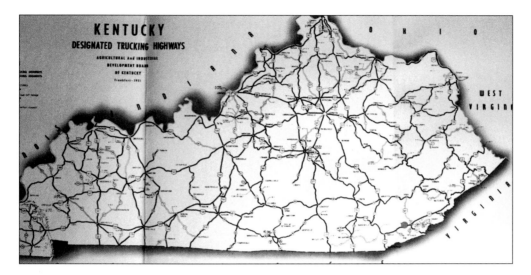

I don't remember that, of course,
but I do remember the summer I was four
and we drove from our house in Kentucky
to California.

In the Pickwick Hotel my daddy held me up
so I could see San Francisco out the window.
But what impressed me more than the cable cars,
more than the bay leading to the ocean,
was the word *Pickwick*.

My hair was in pigtails.
The words were alike, but they were different, too:
   Pickwick — pigtail
I kept saying them over and over to myself,
like you might turn stones in your hand.
I knew they were magic.

How did I know this?
From poems and stories my parents read to me,
from songs my daddy sang,
and from family stories.
For I was also a listening child.

I grew up in Harlan County, Kentucky,
in the same mountain town
with all four of my grandparents,
my mother and father, one brother,
an aunt and uncle, and some cousins, too.

A lot of relatives who didn't live there
came home in the summer to visit.

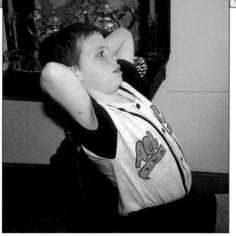

Everybody told stories
around the table,
in the living room,
on front porches,
in the car.
We still do.

One story was about my Grandfather Hoskins
looking after farm animals on a train
bound for Canada. Years later, I told that story
in my book *A Regular Rolling Noah*.

Another family story was
about my Grandmother
Fowler's lost basket.
I wrote a book about
that, too.

Since I loved words and stories, I was naturally
a pretending child. I loved to play "Olden Days"
and "Outer Space." Sometimes my backyard
was a pioneer trail as in *Who Came Down That Road?*

Sometimes it was a village
built inside a cliff,
like the home of the
Anasazi I had visited
out West.
Later I wrote about that
village in *Dreamplace*.

Joey Lyon

And sometimes it was a spaceship,
like I planned to build and ride to the moon.
I tell this story in my book *A Sign*.
Whatever I pretended it was, I could picture the
dangers and imagine what a brave girl would do.
Good practice for a writer!

15

Almost as soon as I learned to make letters,
I became a writing child.
I wanted to draw the words I loved,
to catch the feeling on paper the way
I caught lightning bugs and put them in a jar.
The lightning bugs would die if I didn't
let them go, but I could keep words forever.
My first poem was about a magic bicycle.
I imagined it so hard my eyeballs hurt.
On my tenth birthday, I got a real bicycle.

My first diary was the five-year kind with a key.
I can still smell its smooth shiny leather.
In seventh grade I started writing a novel in code.
Only fifty pages in, I lost my code key
and couldn't read it myself!

When I was fourteen, my
family took a bus tour of
Europe and I kept a journal.
Here's a page from the day
I visited Charles Dickens'
house. I loved his book
A *Christmas Carol.* I've
been keeping journals
ever since.

There are over sixty of them now,
    full of   dreams   jokes   travel stories
     poems   budgets   things my kids say
        story ideas   drawings
descriptions of schools I visit and people I meet there.
Sometimes I even write down the school lunch menu.
My all-time worst? Corn dogs and orange Jell-O®
with peas in it!

How did the third-grade poem-maker
and high school journal-keeper become
a grownup whose books get published?
— by writing, revising, reading, learning
from other writers and teachers,
by not giving up. It took eleven years
to get my first book published.
During that time I had many different jobs.
Today, as I sit working on this book, I'm amazed
and thankful that my job is writing.

My husband is a musician. We both work at home in Lexington, Kentucky. After we get our son, Joey, off to school in the morning, I go up to my writing room.

Steve goes down to his studio. I face blank paper. He faces the piano keyboard, the computer, and the screen. Every day we make things up.

I have cartridge pens I keep in a pen basket.
Each one has a different shade of ink.
When I come to my desk each morning,
I choose a color that feels right and get to work.
I listen for stories in my memory and in my characters.
I pretend, just as I did when I was a child,
but I put all the "acting out" on the page.

At noon, Steve and I go to the gym to exercise.
After that, we come home and have lunch.
Then we go back to work until it's time
to get Joey from school. Some days Joey has
violin lessons or baseball practice. If I take him to
baseball, Steve fixes supper. We take turns with
the laundry and grocery shopping, too.

Our older son Benn lives away from home now,
but he often stops by for a meal or a recording session –
he plays guitar – or a discussion about poetry.

I don't always work at home. Some days
I visit schools and share my creative process.
This is exciting, because I get to meet
young readers and writers.

Teachers often tell me, "My students are happy to do first drafts, but they don't want to revise!" Let me tell you a secret: revision is what makes you a writer. I hardly ever find the right words the first, or third, or even the sixth time. Just like your teacher,  my editor, Dick Jackson, suggests ways to make my writing better. Sometimes we work on a book for years. It takes patience, faith, and a sense of adventure.

Like the house I grew up in, our house is full of books. It is also full of cats. Comet, the oldest, sits on whatever I'm trying to write. Ed sits on what I'm trying to read. And Rosie sits waiting for a bird to fall down the chimney.

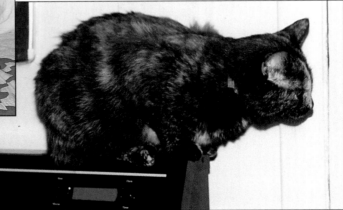

When I was eight, my friend
Paula and I had a cat rescue
service. We would crawl
under houses, climb trees,
poke around attics —
wherever we heard a cat or
kitten was trapped. Nowadays
it's stories I go searching for.
I may have to tramp across
Civil War battlefields as I did
for *Cecil's Story* and *Here and Then*,

or journey deep into a coal mine as I did for
Mama is a Miner. I have to be willing to do
whatever it takes to make the best story I can.

Not all of this work will lead to books.
My writing room is full of rejected manuscripts.
It's hard when I put my heart into something
and no one wants to publish it. But I learn
from the process. And since I love writing itself,
I am willing to go back to my desk
and try again to find the magic in the words.

I didn't always want to be a writer.
First I wanted to be a neon sign-maker,
then a tightrope walker, a rocket scientist,
a veterinarian, a folksinger.

But all the time I was imagining those things,
I was keeping journals, making poems.

One day, halfway through college, I was thinking about my life's work. I asked myself, "Of all the things you do, what gives you the most joy?" The answer was writing.

George Ella Lyon

Other Books by George Ella Lyon

A B Cedar: An Alphabet of Trees; Borrowed Children; Come a Tide; Here and Then; The Outside Inn

About the Photographer

Ann Olson is a freelance writer and photographer. She took photographs as slides for the first time when she and her husband Frank lived in Alaska twenty-five years ago. Several years later, Ann moved to eastern Kentucky where she and Frank raised their son and daughter as well as some goats, chickens, dogs, and cats. When she was growing up in Connecticut, Ann had a five-year diary like George Ella's. She never imagined then that she would someday be in a writing group with George Ella and four other Kentucky friends.

Acknowledgments

Photographs on title page, pages 4, 7, 9, 10, 11, 12, 14, 16, and 17 courtesy of George Ella Lyon. On page 5, map of Kentucky from *Economic Atlas of Kentucky*, Volume 1, Agricultural and Industrial Development Board, Frankfort, 1951, and "Interstate Route Map" of the western United States from Esso Standard Oil Co. Copyright 1952, used by permission of American Map Co. Photograph on page 6 of Pickwick Hotel by Robert Lee Brown, Jr. Drawing on page 15 by Joey Lyon. Photograph of Richard Jackson on page 25 courtesy of Sandra Jordan. Illustration on page 11 from *A Regular Rolling Noah* by George Ella Lyon, illustrated by Stephen Gammell. Illustrations copyright 1986 by Stephen Gammell. Publisher Bradbury Press. Reprinted by permission of Macmillan, Inc. Illustration on page 12 from *Basket* by George Ella Lyon, illustrated by Mary Szilagyi. Illustrations copyright 1990 by Mary Szilagyi. Reprinted by permission of the publisher, Orchard Books, New York. Illustration on page 13 from *Who Came Down That Road* by George Ella Lyon, illustrated by Peter Catalanotto. Illustrations copyright 1992 by Peter Catalanotto. Reprinted by permission of the publisher, Orchard Books, New York. Illustration on page 14 from *Dreamplace* by George Ella Lyon, illustrated by Peter Catalanotto. Illustrations copyright 1993 by Peter Catalanotto. Reprinted by permission of the publisher, Orchard Books, New York. Illustration on page 28 from *Cecil's Story* by George Ella Lyon, illustrated by Peter Catalanatto. Illustrations copyright 1992 by Peter Catalanotto. Reprinted by permission of the publisher, Orchard Books, New York. Photograph of Ann Olson by Lori Spear.